Mountain Rescues: Tales of Courage for Kids

I
The Lost Trail,

Chapter 1: The Lost Trail

Once upon a time, in the magical land of Mountainside, there was a brave group of animal friends who loved to explore. They were called the Adventure Squad. One sunny morning, they decided to embark on a thrilling journey along the mysterious Lost Trail.

Led by their fearless leader, Max the Bear, the Adventure Squad set off with excitement in their hearts. The trail was hidden deep within the dense forest, filled with tall trees and chirping birds. As they ventured deeper, the air grew cooler, and the sound of rushing water filled their ears.

But suddenly, disaster struck! The mischievous wind blew a strong gust, causing the leaves to rustle loudly and the trail to disappear before their eyes. The friends were lost!

Frantically, they searched for clues, following their instincts. They came across a sparkling river and decided to follow its gentle flow. Through thick bushes and over mossy rocks, they continued their quest.

As they traveled, they encountered friendly creatures who offered help and shared stories of the trail's magical secrets. With renewed hope, the Adventure Squad pressed on, their determination unwavering.

After a long and thrilling adventure, they finally discovered a hidden path, shimmering with golden sunlight. It led them back to the trail they had lost. Cheers of joy echoed through the mountains as the friends reunited with the familiar path.

With their spirits lifted and the lessons of perseverance learned, the Adventure Squad continued their exploration, eager to unravel the mysteries of Mountainside.

And so, their incredible journey began, filled with bravery, friendship, and the wonders of nature. Little did they know that more extraordinary adventures awaited them on the Lost Trail.

II
A Cry for Help,

Once upon a time, in the magical land of Mountainville, there lived a group of adventurous animal friends. They loved exploring the mountains and going on exciting journeys together. In the previous chapter, "The Lost Trail," the animal friends embarked on a thrilling adventure to find a hidden treasure.

Now, in Chapter 2, "A Cry for Help," our friends were enjoying a sunny day in the mountains when they heard a faint cry for help echoing through the valleys. Curious and concerned, they followed the sound, hopping over rocks and running through the tall grass.

As they reached the source of the cry, they discovered a young mountain goat named Billy. Poor Billy had slipped and gotten stuck on a narrow ledge, unable to find his way back up. The animal friends quickly gathered around, determined to help their new friend.

First, Rabbit used her speedy hops to bring back a sturdy branch. Together, they created a makeshift ladder to reach Billy. Squirrel, with her nimble paws, carefully guided Billy's hooves onto the ladder. With the combined efforts of all the friends, they slowly and steadily pulled Billy back to safety.

Exhausted but relieved, Billy thanked the animal friends for their bravery and kindness. They reassured him that helping others in need was what friends do. With smiles on their faces, they continued their journey through the mountains, ready for more adventures and new friends to meet.

And so, the animal friends learned an important lesson about friendship and lending a helping hand in "A Cry for Help." Little did they know that more exciting challenges awaited them in the chapters to come.

III
Brave Climbers Unite,

Once upon a time, in a land of majestic mountains, there lived a group of brave climbers. These climbers loved exploring the rocky peaks and were always ready for an adventure. One sunny day, as they gathered at their favorite mountain spot, they noticed something unusual.

A cry for help echoed through the air, catching their attention. The climbers looked around, trying to locate the source of the sound. And there, on a steep ledge high above them, they spotted a young bird, trembling with fear.

Without hesitation, the brave climbers united in their mission to save the frightened bird. They knew it would be a challenging climb, but their determination was unwavering. With ropes, helmets, and sturdy boots, they began their ascent.

Step by step, they carefully climbed, encouraging each other along the way. The wind whispered through their hair as they neared the ledge. Finally, they reached the spot where the bird perched, its wings trembling.

With gentle hands, one of the climbers reached out and carefully cradled the bird. It chirped softly, expressing its gratitude. The climbers smiled and felt a sense of accomplishment. They had successfully completed their mission.

Together, they descended the mountain, the rescued bird nestled safely in their hands. As they reached the base, a crowd had gathered, amazed by their bravery and teamwork. The climbers shared their story, inspiring others to be brave and lend a helping hand whenever they could.

And so, the brave climbers united in their love for adventure and their commitment to helping those in need. Little did they know that their next journey would lead them to even greater heights and more daring rescues. But that, my young friends, is a story for another day.

IV
Rescuing a Feathered Friend,

Chapter 4: Rescuing a Feathered Friend

Once upon a time, high up in the mountains, a group of brave climbers embarked on an exciting adventure. They had heard a little bird's cry for help echoing through the peaks. Determined to rescue their feathered friend, they set out on a daring mission.

With ropes and climbing gear, the climbers scaled rocky cliffs and crossed narrow bridges. The air was crisp and filled with anticipation as they followed the sound of the bird's sweet chirps. They encountered slippery slopes and gusty winds, but their determination never wavered.

After a long and treacherous climb, they reached a ledge where they found the little bird perched on a tree branch. It was a colorful parrot with vibrant feathers that shimmered in the sunlight. The bird seemed scared and unable to fly.

One of the climbers, named Sam, gently approached the parrot. "Don't worry, little friend," he said softly. "We're here to help you." Sam carefully reached out his hand, and the parrot hopped onto his finger.

Together, the climbers devised a plan. They built a makeshift nest using leaves and twigs, creating a safe place for the bird to rest. They took turns feeding it seeds and drops of water from their canteens.

Days turned into weeks as they patiently nursed the parrot back to health. They named it Rainbow, inspired by its vibrant plumage. Rainbow soon became a cherished member of their mountaineering family.

With Rainbow by their side, the climbers continued their journey, facing new challenges and discovering breathtaking vistas. And as they climbed higher, their bond grew stronger.

Little did they know that their adventures were just beginning. What other incredible rescues awaited them in the majestic mountains? Only time would tell.

To be continued...

(Note: This is a fictional story written for children and may not reflect real-life mountain climbing scenarios.)

V
The Mountain's Secret Cave,

Once upon a time, in a beautiful land surrounded by tall mountains, there was a group of adventurous friends named Timmy, Lily, and their loyal dog, Buddy. One sunny day, they decided to explore the mountains and see what secrets they held.

As they climbed higher and higher, they stumbled upon a hidden cave tucked away between two giant rocks. Curiosity sparkled in their eyes as they entered the dark, mysterious cave. Inside, they discovered a magical sight – glowing crystals that illuminated the walls, creating a breathtaking display.

Excitedly, they ventured deeper into the cave, their laughter echoing through the narrow passages. Suddenly, they heard a soft chirping sound. They followed the sound and discovered a tiny, injured bird with a broken wing. It was a colorful parrot named Polly.

Filled with compassion, the brave climbers gently cradled Polly in their hands and decided to help her. They fashioned a cozy nest using leaves and moss, creating a safe place for Polly to rest and heal. Timmy and Lily took turns feeding her small bits of fruit and water, hoping she would regain her strength.

Days turned into weeks, and with their tender care, Polly's wing began to mend. She chirped happily, grateful for the friends who had rescued her. One sunny morning, when the time was right, they brought Polly back to the entrance of the cave.

With a flap of her wings, Polly soared into the sky, bidding them a fond farewell. Timmy, Lily, and Buddy watched in awe as Polly disappeared into the clouds. They knew that their act of kindness had made a difference in Polly's life.

As they made their way down the mountain, the friends smiled, knowing they had discovered not only the mountain's secret cave but also the power of friendship and the joy of helping others. Little did they know that more exciting adventures awaited them in the mountains, filled with bravery, compassion, and the spirit of exploration.

VI
Racing Against Time,

Once upon a time, in a beautiful land surrounded by tall mountains, there was a group of adventurous friends named Timmy, Lily, and their loyal dog, Buddy. One sunny day, they decided to explore the mountains and see what secrets they held.

As they climbed higher and higher, they stumbled upon a hidden cave tucked away between two giant rocks. Curiosity sparkled in their eyes as they entered the dark, mysterious cave. Inside, they discovered a magical sight – glowing crystals that illuminated the walls, creating a breathtaking display.

Excitedly, they ventured deeper into the cave, their laughter echoing through the narrow passages. Suddenly, they heard a soft chirping sound. They followed the sound and discovered a tiny, injured bird with a broken wing. It was a colorful parrot named Polly.

Filled with compassion, the brave climbers gently cradled Polly in their hands and decided to help her. They fashioned a cozy nest using leaves and moss, creating a safe place for Polly to rest and heal. Timmy and Lily took turns feeding her small bits of fruit and water, hoping she would regain her strength.

Days turned into weeks, and with their tender care, Polly's wing began to mend. She chirped happily, grateful for the friends who had rescued her. One sunny morning, when the time was right, they brought Polly back to the entrance of the cave.

With a flap of her wings, Polly soared into the sky, bidding them a fond farewell. Timmy, Lily, and Buddy watched in awe as Polly disappeared into the clouds. They knew that their act of kindness had made a difference in Polly's life.

As they made their way down the mountain, the friends smiled, knowing they had discovered not only the mountain's secret cave but also the power of friendship and the joy of helping others. Little did they know that more exciting adventures awaited them in the mountains, filled with bravery, compassion, and the spirit of exploration.

VII
A Bridge of Courage,

Chapter 7: A Bridge of Courage

Once upon a time, in the heart of the majestic mountains, there was a group of brave friends named Timmy, Lily, and Sammy. They loved exploring and going on exciting adventures together.

One sunny day, they stumbled upon a deep ravine with a rushing river flowing beneath. They wanted to cross to the other side, but there was no bridge in sight. The only way to reach their destination was to find a way to build a bridge.

With determination in their hearts, Timmy, Lily, and Sammy gathered branches, rocks, and vines. They worked together, using their creative minds and problem- solving skills, to construct a bridge. It wasn't easy, but they persevered, knowing that their friendship and bravery would guide them.

As the bridge took shape, doubts began to creep into their minds. What if the bridge wasn't strong enough? What if it collapsed under their weight? But they didn't let fear hold them back. They believed in their abilities and trusted that their bridge would hold.

Finally, the bridge was complete—a beautiful, sturdy structure spanning the ravine. Timmy, Lily, and Sammy took a deep breath, held hands, and took their first step onto the bridge. With each step, their courage grew stronger, and their fears melted away.

They crossed the bridge together, filled with pride and joy. On the other side, they discovered a hidden treasure—a secret meadow with vibrant flowers and playful animals. Their hearts danced with happiness, knowing that their bravery had led them to this magical place.

From that day forward, Timmy, Lily, and Sammy cherished their bridge of courage. They knew that with determination, teamwork, and a little bit of bravery, they could conquer any challenge that lay ahead.

And so, their adventures continued, with the bridge serving as a symbol of their friendship and the limitless possibilities that awaited them in the mountains.

The End

VIII
The Power of Teamwork,

Chapter 8: The Power of Teamwork

Once upon a time, in the beautiful mountains, there lived a group of animal friends. There was Benny the bear, Daisy the deer, Ricky the rabbit, and Sammy the squirrel. They loved playing together and exploring the forest.

One sunny day, they heard a loud noise coming from the top of the mountain. They followed the sound and discovered that a big rock had blocked the path to their favorite meadow. They wanted to go there to have a picnic and play games, but the rock was too heavy for any of them to move alone.

Determined to reach their special spot, the animal friends decided to work together. Benny used his strong paws to push from one side, while Daisy pushed with her antlers from the other. Ricky hopped around, giving them encouragement, and Sammy scurried up the trees to find a rope.

With everyone's help, they tied the rope around the rock and pulled with all their might. Slowly, the rock started to move, and the path became clear once again. The animal friends cheered with joy!

Their teamwork didn't end there. They held hands as they carefully crossed a rickety old bridge, supporting each other and making sure everyone felt safe. They learned that by working together, they could overcome any obstacle.

As they finally reached the meadow, the animal friends spread out their picnic blanket and enjoyed a delicious feast. They laughed, played, and felt grateful for the power of teamwork.

From that day forward, Benny, Daisy, Ricky, and Sammy knew that they could achieve anything when they worked together. Their friendship grew even stronger, and they continued to explore the mountains, knowing that their bond would always guide them.

The end.

IX
The Little Hero,

Once upon a time, in a beautiful mountain village, there lived a little boy named Timmy. Timmy was just five years old, but he had a heart full of bravery and kindness. One sunny day, as Timmy was exploring the forest near his home, he heard a faint cry for help.

Curiosity sparked in Timmy's eyes as he followed the sound. The cry led him to a small clearing, where he found a tiny bird with a broken wing. The poor bird looked scared and helpless.

Without a second thought, Timmy gently scooped up the bird and cradled it in his hands. He knew he had to help this little feathered friend. Timmy ran back to his house, where his parents had a cozy nest for injured animals.

Timmy's mom and dad were amazed by his courage and quick thinking. They gently placed the bird in the nest and wrapped its wing with a soft bandage. Timmy named the bird Buddy, and they became the best of friends.

Together, Timmy and Buddy spent their days playing and exploring. Timmy learned how to feed Buddy and make him comfortable. He discovered that Buddy loved to sing cheerful songs, filling their home with joy.

As days turned into weeks, Buddy's wing healed, and he grew stronger. One sunny morning, when the forest was filled with chirping birds, Buddy spread his wings and took flight. Timmy watched with a proud smile as Buddy soared through the sky, free and happy.

Timmy knew he had become a little hero, saving Buddy's life and teaching him to be strong. From that day forward, Timmy felt a special bond with animals, always ready to lend a helping hand.

And so, Timmy's story of bravery and compassion spread throughout the mountain village, inspiring others to be heroes too. Because even the smallest acts of kindness can make a big difference in the world.

X
Celebrating Victories

Chapter 10: Celebrating Victories

Once upon a time, in a land of majestic mountains, there were a group of brave adventurers who loved to explore and conquer new heights. They had faced many challenges and had overcome them with their determination and courage. Now, it was time for them to celebrate their victories!

The adventurers gathered together at the foot of the tallest mountain. They set up a colorful picnic with delicious treats like sandwiches, fruits, and cupcakes. Laughter filled the air as they shared stories of their daring escapades and the obstacles they had overcome.

They played games, like tug-of-war and sack races, to show off their strength and agility. The little hero of the group, a young boy named Timmy, was especially praised for his bravery throughout their journey. He blushed with pride as his friends cheered for him.

As the sun began to set, painting the sky in shades of pink and orange, the adventurers lit a bonfire. They sat around it, singing songs and roasting marshmallows. The warmth of the fire matched the warmth of their friendship.

They reminisced about the challenges they had faced together and how they had supported each other every step of the way. They realized that it was their unity and teamwork that had led them to victory.

With hearts full of gratitude and joy, the adventurers made a promise to continue their adventures and face new challenges together. They knew that with their friendship and determination, there was no limit to what they could achieve.

And so, under the starry night sky, they danced and celebrated their victories, grateful for the memories they had made and the bonds they had formed.

The End

Fin.

Printed in Great Britain
by Amazon